This book
belongs to:

~~[name crossed out]~~

~~[name crossed out]~~
~~[name crossed out]~~
~~[name crossed out]~~

First Published 1998
by Hodder Children's Books,
a division of Hodder Headline Limited
338 Euston Road, London NW1 3BH

Text and illustrations copyright © Mick Inkpen 1998

10 9 8 7 6
ISBN 0340 70381 4 (PB)

A CIP catalogue record for this book
is available from the British Library

The right of Mick Inkpen to be identfied
as the author of this work has been asserted by him
in accordance with the Copyright, Designs and Patents Act 1988.

Manufactured in China by Imago

The
Great Pet Sale

Mick Inkpen

Hodder
Children's
Books

A division of Hodder Headline Limited

'EVERYTHING MUST GO!'
said the sign on the pet shop
window.

In the window was a rat.
I looked at him. Half of his
whiskers were missing.
'I'm a bargain!'
called the rat
through the glass.

'I'm only 1 p!
Choose me!'

Inside the shop there was

a tiny terrapin for 2 pence,

a turtle for 3 pence
and a tortoise,
a great big one,

for 4 pence.

'I'm sure you wouldn't like one of THOSE!' said the rat. 'But you'd like me. . .

THINGS
BEGINNING
WITH 'P'
5P
EACH

On the perch were,
'THINGS BEGINNING
WITH P'.
A pelican,
a puffin,
a penguin,
a parrot
and a platypus!

All 5 pence each.

'Oh, you don't want
anything beginning
with P!' said the rat.
'R! . . . R is what
you want!
R for Ratty!'

SALAMANDER 6p
SKINK 7p
GECKO 8p

Behind a plastic rock was
a salamander for 6 pence,
a skink for 7 pence
and a gecko for 8 pence.

'Which one is which?'
I said.
'Nobody knows!
Nobody cares!' said
the rat.
'Sausages on legs!
You don't want
one of THOSE!'

9p
THE PAIR

The next two animals were,

'**9**P THE PAIR'.

'Who wants a koala that doesn't like leaves?' said the rat. 'Or an anteater that won't eat its ant?

I'm not fussy!

I'll eat. . .

. . . ANYTHING!'

ASSORTED
LITTLE
BROWN
CREATURES

In the cardboard box were,
'Assorted Little Brown Creatures,
10 Pence the Lot'.

'Boring! Boring! Boring!'
said the rat. 'I'm not boring!
Look! I can stand on one leg!'
And it did.

At the back of the shop we came to a big door.

'What's in there?' I said.

'Oh, just a dragon,' said the rat.

'There's no such thing,' I said.

'Then you won't want one, will you!' said the rat.

I opened the door. It was a dragon. A great, big Komodo Dragon for **25** pence!

At last the rat was quiet.
'You're not going to
choose me, are you?'
it said sadly.
'Shhh!' I said.
'I've made up
my mind.'

I counted my money.

£1.00 exactly.

It was just enough
to buy the rat. . .

. . . and everything else in the shop!

Other books by Mick Inkpen